Published in 1990 by Magi Publications,
in association with Star Books International, 55 Crowland Avenue, Hayes, Middx UB3 4JP
First published in 1987 by Editions Fleurus, Paris, France, with the title "Kitou Scrogneugneu".

Printed and bound in Belgium

© Editions Fleurus, 1987

ISBN 1 85430 191 8

SCRUFFY SCROGGLES

by Ann Rocard

illustrated by Marino Degano

Magi Publications, London

Once upon a time in Lilyville, there lived a family of monsters, the Scroggles. They were the most horrible monsters, hideous and slobbery, with six eyes, and they lived under the local park. They only came out at night, so people passing at a late hour sometimes imagined seeing strange shadows among the trees.

But they were not imagining things! It was the Scroggles coming out of their tunnel, by the first prickly bush past the adventure playground, marching in single file behind Gruesome Gresham, the father monster. There was Frightful Flavia, the mother monster, Revolting Ronald, the grandfather monster, Nasty Nelly, the daughter monster... and trailing along behind came Scruffy, a very small monster indeed.

"Hurry up, Scruffy!" growled his father.
"What a trial that child is!" sighed his mother.
"Little monsters did as they were told in
my young day," grumbled his grandfather.
"Brothers are beastly!" said his sister, nastily.

Scruffy sighed and shrugged his shoulders. He didn't like slashing car tyres, and breaking windows was boring. Gruesome Gresham expected his son to become the most dreadful monster in the world. Scruffy wanted to do as he was told, but being monstrous was very tiring!

While the family wreaked havoc along Station Road, Scruffy waited. He heard someone crying, and looking up, he saw a little girl through a lighted window.

"Poor thing," thought Scruffy, "I wonder if I could help her?"

But there was no time to think about that, as Nasty Nelly started dragging him along by the hair.

"Shuffle more when you walk!" said his father.

"Pick your nose at once!" said his mother.

"NEVER use a hankie!" commanded his grandfather.

"Brothers are beastly!" said Nasty Nelly, nastily.

The fact is, as a monster, Scruffy was a failure. He was always bottom of the class at school. He never made any spelling mistakes, he never got his sums wrong, and worst of all, he NEVER cheated.

Every day the teacher made Scruffy stand in the corner, while all the other little monsters made fun of him. "Scruffy is a duffer! Yah boo Scruffy."

One day the headmonster called Scruffy to her office. "Who wants a hard-working little monster like you in school? You're expelled."

So Scruffy didn't go to school any more. He stopped learning how to tear up exercise books and get sums wrong, and started enjoying himself at home, reading books and drawing pretty coloured flowers.

"You're wasting your time," his mother told him. "Monsters shouldn't read. It puts ideas into their heads!"

His father agreed. "Who taught you to draw pretty flowers? Disgusting! Why don't you draw vipers, venomous spiders and slimy dragons instead?"

That evening, Scruffy felt very sad.

"I'm sick of my family. I wish they would go away, so I'd never ever have to see them again." Scruffy began to cry green and yellow monster tears. He was so tired of being scolded and smacked that he decided to go that very night and visit the little girl in the window.

A little later, Gruesome Gresham was leading the Scroggles in single file through the town. He was in a vile temper.

"Hurry up, Scruffy!" he growled.

"What a trial that child is!" groaned his mother.

"Little monsters did as they were told in my young day," grumbled his grandfather.

"Brothers are beastly!" said Nasty Nelly, without bothering to turn round.

But Scruffy wasn't there any more. He had hidden himself behind a dustbin.

"Phew!" he breathed. "They haven't noticed I'm missing!"

When the coast was clear, Scruffy made for Station Road. There was no light on in the window, but he could hear the sound of crying.

He piled up several dustbins, then climbed onto the very top one and peered through the window.

The little girl was sitting on her bed, sniffling.

"I don't want to go to sleep!" she wailed. "I'm thirsty and I want a drink! I'm sick of my family. I wish they would go away so I'd never ever have to see them again."

Scruffy was astonished. Fancy someone else feeling the same way he did! He knocked softly on the window. The little girl came over, looking very surprised.

"What are you doing there?" she asked.

"Watching you," said Scruffy.

The little girl made a face. "You look really horrible!" she said.

"Horrible, hideous and slobbery, and I've got six eyes in my hair," said Scruffy proudly. "My name is Scruffy Scroggles. Pleased to meet you."

"Mine's Lucy," said the little girl. "Welcome to my room."

Lucy and Scruffy talked and talked until sunrise. Lucy told Scruffy how unhappy she was, and how nasty her parents were to her.

"I'm sure they don't mean to be nasty," said Scruffy.

"But you've left *your* family," Lucy pointed out.

"Ah, but I'm a monster," said Scruffy.

"I wish you'd stay here," Lucy whispered in Scruffy's ear.

Scruffy hesitated for a moment. "I'm afraid I'm a very badly behaved monster."

"You seem very well behaved to me," said Lucy. "What do you do wrong?"

"I never pick my nose," Scruffy explained.

"I always do," said Lucy.

"I always put my hand in front of my mouth when I cough or sneeze," Scruffy continued.

"I never do," said Lucy.

"I don't put my elbows on the table at mealtimes," added Scruffy.

"Oh, I do!" said Lucy.

"I never stick my tongue out, and I never say rude things," went on the little monster.

"I do! I do! I do!" said Lucy, bursting out laughing. Scruffy was so funny!

Lucy took Scruffy's paw.

"Look," she said, "I'm going to hide you in a suitcase under my bed. It will be our secret."

"It looks even more comfortable than my old burrow," said Scruffy.

Suddenly, Lucy felt very tired. She got into her bed, and Scruffy scrambled into his hiding place. Outside, Station Road was bathed in sunlight. Indoors, the two friends were fast asleep.

And what about the other Scroggles?
After searching all over town for Scruffy, they
went back to the park.

"Good riddance!" growled Gruesome Gresham.

"What a trial that child was!" sighed
Frightful Flavia.

"Little monsters didn't get lost in my young
day," said Revolting Ronald.

"Brothers really are the very end!" said Nasty
Nelly, cackling nastily.

Next day, the four of them packed their
suitcases and left town.

Nothing was ever heard of them again.

However, there is still one monster in town. A very small monster, horrible, hideous and slobbery, with six eyes. He lives in a suitcase in Station Road.

He has taught Lucy not to pick her nose, and Lucy has taught him the rudest words she knows: "Cogglewoggle pibblywibbly pong!"

But whatever you do, don't say them!

Even if, some day, you think you see the shadow of a little monster in the moonlight, in Lilyville Park, you mustn't say them. No one must ever know that Scruffy Scroggles is best friends with Lucy, and lives in a suitcase under her bed.